To Brian, love always xx - LS

For Mum & Dad - FL

SIMON & SCHUSTER
First published in Great Britain in 2018 by
Simon & Schuster UK Ltd, 1st Floor, 222 Gray's Inn Road,
London WC1X 8HB • A CBS Company • Text copyright © 2018 Linda Sarah
Illustrations copyright © 2018 Fiona Lumbers • The right of Linda Sarah and
Fiona Lumbers to be identified as the author and illustrator of this work has
been asserted by them in accordance with the Copyright, Designs and Patents
Act, 1988 • All rights reserved, including the right of reproduction in whole
or in part in any form • A CIP catalogue record for this book is available from
the British Library upon request
ISBN: 978-1-4711-1925-5 (HB) • ISBN: 978-1-4711-1926-2 (PB)
ISBN: 978-1-4711-1927-9 (eBook)

THE SECRET SKY GARDEN

Linda Sarah and Fiona Lumbers

SIMON & SCHUSTER
London   New York   Sydney   Toronto   New Delhi

Funni liked the old airport car park.

It hadn't been used for years
and was greyer than a Monday sky.

But Funni loved being there,
hearing the planes take off and touch down,
while the blue rooftops stretched
for miles like a calm, still sea.

She came there most Saturdays,

sometimes with her
Kestrel Warrior stunt kite,

sometimes with
her recorder.

But something was missing.

Definitely.

She'd learnt to play the sounds around -
notes from the tannoy in the terminal,

the high-low whine of planes
coming in to land,

and the music of bells in City Square.

But something was missing.

Definitely.

So she hatched a plan.

Each Saturday Funni lugged up a huge sack of soil, cleaned the carpet of litter, swept the drift of squished cans and other left-behinds.

After three months of Saturdays,
she gently nuzzled seeds into the soil
that now completely covered the rooftop car park.

It was Zoo who first noticed,
coming in to land on his flight home from Dad's.

WOW! He grinned bigger than in three months.
"I've got to go there," he thought . . .

. . . a garden, there, in the air,

full of flowers, bright like an emperor's blanket,
nodding and waving - hello!

Funni watered her flowers,

flew her fierce kite,

played a new song she'd learnt
from a tiny, red radio
found in a stairwell.

But something
was still missing.

Definitely.

That feeling.
Like an ache, a hole,
not a full-up, satisfied feeling you get
when you're happy and there's the warm buzz
of home and someone laughing in another room.

And that's when Zoo arrived, grinning shyly.

He told her how amazing her car park garden
looked from way up there.
"It's awesome! I saw it and thought
I must be dreaming!"

And it turns out
they both flew kites.

Zoo's was shaped
like a shield.

He also played a silver harmonica and
could soon play all the sounds around -

the notes of the tannoy,
the descending hum,

the chiming bells.

And as the sky darkens,
when you're coming in to land,
you might notice some bright sparks

- maybe fairy lights, maybe fireworks.

And if you come closer,
you might hear a whole city of sounds
being played by two friends,

their kites criss-crossing
in the secret sky garden.

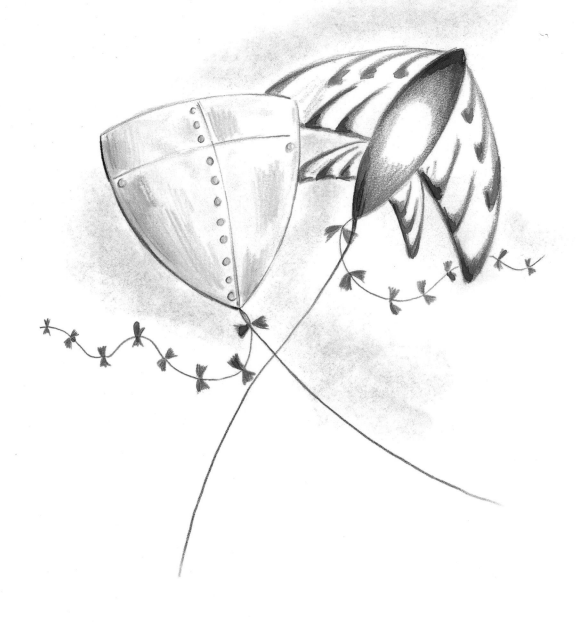